Steadman Squirrel and The School Dance

Written by Jeffrey Roy Ford
Illustrations by Mike Motz

I dedicate this book
to all my family and friends.

Steadman Squirrel and The School Dance
© 2021 Jeffrey Roy Ford. All Rights reserved.
No part of this publication may be reproduced or transmitted in any form
or by any means, electronic, mechanical, including photocopy,
recording, or any information storage and retrieval system,
without permission in writing from the author.

Steadman Squirrel and The School Dance

Written by **Jeffrey Roy Ford**

Illustrations by **Mike Motz**

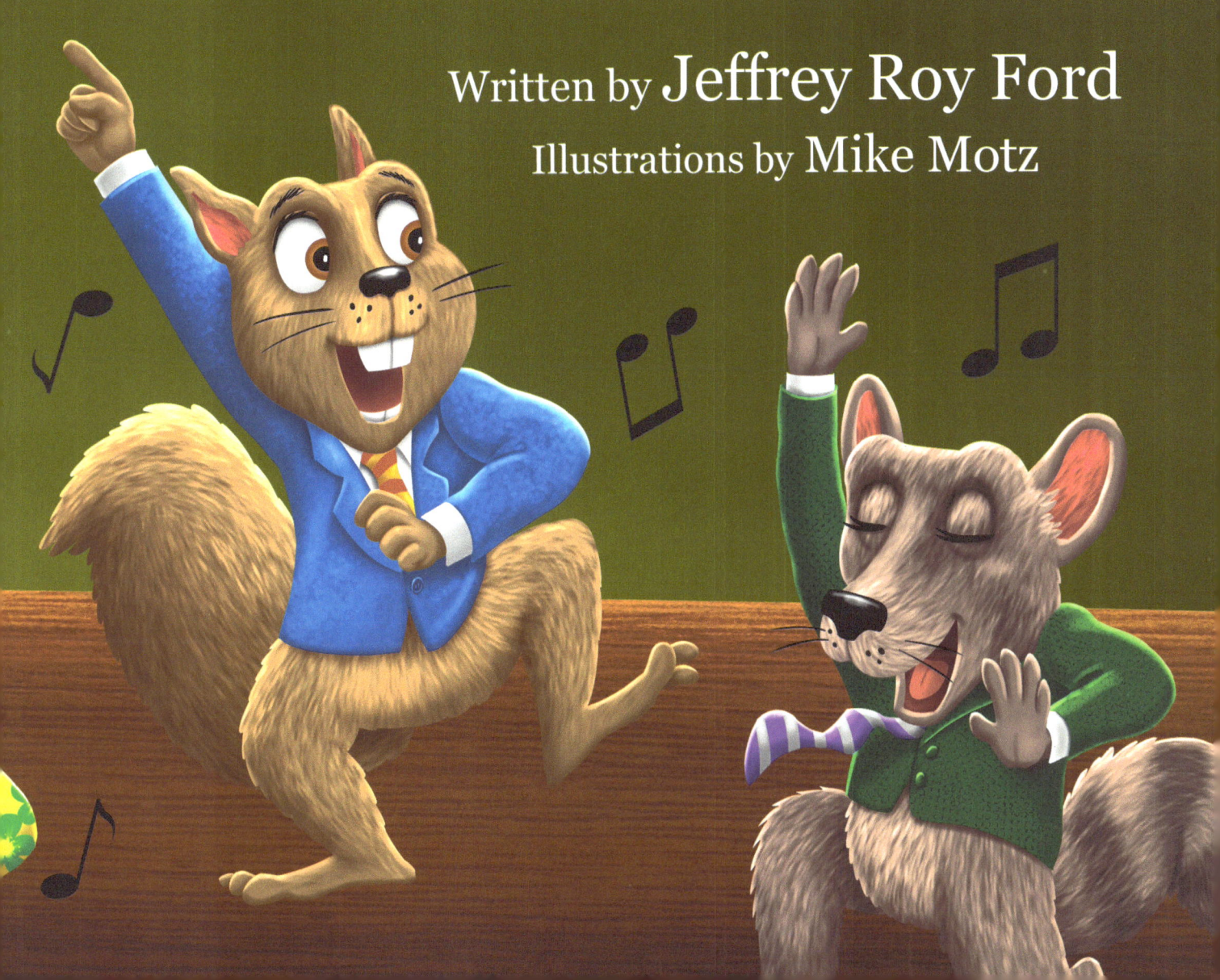

"It's almost time for the dance, Steadman!" Momma Squirrel says.

"Okay, Momma," Steadman replies.

Steadman stands in front of the mirror in his new blue suit and shakes his hips while wiggling his fuzzy brown tail on the soft rug in his bedroom as he practices his moves for the school dance tonight.

Steadman goes into the kitchen where Grandma Squirrel is eating a big bowl of acorn stew. He sits next to her at the long wooden dinner table and puts his head down on it.

"What's the matter, Steadman?" Grandma Squirrel asks.

"The school dance is tonight, and I want to go on the dance floor and dance. I'm scared I will dance badly, and the other kids will make fun of me. Rema Rabbit will be there," Steadman responds.

"Believe in yourself, Steadman. You can do anything that you put your mind to," Grandma Squirrel says.

Papa Squirrel runs into the kitchen, holding a soapy sponge as he chases Stewart, Steadman's filthy little brother, through the room, trying to get him clean. "Please take those dirty pajamas off and get in the tub like your brother, Steadman, did earlier," he begs.

A short while later, Steadman and Stewart, dressed in their matching blue suits, frolic out of their treehouse and down the oak tree.

"Slow down, Stewart, we can't get dirty," Steadman cautions.

They enter Freshy Forest, where they meet Rashawn Racoon and Rema Rabbit by the apple trees. Rashawn looks fantastic in his green suit, and Rema is beautiful in her long, pink dress. They all high paw each other as they walk by the cherry bushes and down the nature trail.

The children walk by Professor Ozello Owl, who is playing checkers against Dr. Billy Bobcat on a tree stump by Freshy River.

Professor Ozello Owl jumps Dr. Billy Bobcat's last red piece. "Give up, Billy! You will never beat me," he laughs.

"No matter how many times I lose, I will never give up on my goal of winning," Dr. Billy Bobcat responds.

The children arrive at Banana Nut Creek Elementary School's gymnasium. The gym floor is full of students talking and dancing.

Paxton Possum is on the big brown stage flicking his banjo, while his brother Pernell Possum hits the bongo drums, creating a delightful tune.

"Oink! Oink! Stewart, get off the basketball rim!" Principal Pandra Pig yells.

Steadman shakes his head, hoping his little brother will stop acting up.

Many of the students form a large circle, clapping and singing as each of them takes turns dancing in the center of it.

Rashawn gets into the circle and jumps up and down to the beat of the bongo drums.

Next, Rema enters it, hopping and smiling as the banjo's music makes her smile. "It's your turn, Steadman!" she exclaims.

Steadman's eyes grow wide, and his heart starts beating fast as he sees all the students staring at him. He sprints out of the gymnasium and runs to the school's baseball field.

His teacher, Mr. Dorian Dog, catches up to him. "Woof! Woof! Wait, Steadman! What's wrong?"

As tears pour down his furry face, Steadman turns to his teacher. "I want to dance, but I'm scared that everyone is going to make fun of me."

"Steadman, do not let fear stop you from achieving anything you want to achieve in your life. Believe in yourself and go after all your dreams and goals. You never know what you can do until you try," Mr. Dorian Dog replies.

Steadman thinks about what his teacher just said, and he goes back into the gymnasium and jumps into the center of the dance circle. He closes his eyes, shakes his hips, and wiggles his tail to the sweet music of the banjo and the bongo drum. Finally, he opens his eyes, and the other students are clapping as they cheer him on.

"Go, Steadman! Go, Steadman!" all the students shout.

Steadman smiles. "I did it. I faced my fears, and I accomplished my goal!"

The End

Meet
Jeffrey Roy Ford

Jeffrey Roy Ford is an animal lover and former substitute teacher. He has dedicated his life to making a difference by using his love for animals to create fun stories that teach children important life lessons.

CPSIA information can be obtained
at www.ICGtesting.com
Printed in the USA
LVHW081914030423
743357LV00002B/23

Made in the USA
Coppell, TX
06 October 2024

The end.

The friend said, "Oh, I don't care. I LOVE bananas!"
Pita smiled widely as she was finally chosen for snack. She learned that she didn't need to change at all. She just needed to be her bright banana self.

The little boy said, "Oh, yes. But it's been in the bowl for quite a while."

"Why has it been there so long?" the friend asked.

The little boy responded, "Oh, I just don't like bananas. Are you sure you want it? It looks bruised."

Finally, the friend said, "Hey, I think there's a banana at the bottom of the fruit bowl. Can I choose the banana for my snack?"

But today was different. The little boy had a friend come over to play and the friend peered into the blue bowl to choose his snack. Pita still sat glumly at the bottom of the bowl as the friend looked at all of his choices.

She heard the boy's mother say, "Choose a snack from the fruit bowl" and she saw the little boy reach in and choose a new red apple.

Pita was still sitting sadly at the bottom of the blue bowl when snack time came. The fruits were buzzing excitedly but she wasn't paying attention. She still felt sore and her peel hurt and she missed her special sticker.

Pita was not surprised. She was dull and bruised now. That night, she didn't try to jump out of the fruit bowl. She just sat sadly at the bottom of the blue bowl, unable to sleep.

"Of course," said his mother. She opened a cabinet and then brought over a new group of fruits for the boy to choose from. He promptly chose a purple plum.

The little boy peered into the blue bowl and stared at the banana before asking his mother, "Do we have any other choices?"

"Choose your snack from the bowl," the mother said.

The next afternoon, when snack time came, Pita was tired and sore and sad but she waited anxiously for the boy and his mother to come to the cozy kitchen.

That night, she barely slept. Her peel didn't feel good after all of the shining, and she was sore from the squishing. She missed her sticker. But she was sure the next day the boy would choose her for a snack. After all, she was all alone in the fruit bowl.

One little tear fell down her cheek as she pulled her beloved sticker off, hopped out of the fruit bowl and threw it in the nearby garbage can.

She was alone in the fruit bowl now, wondering why the little boy didn't want to choose her. She was fiddling with her sticker when it dawned on her. None of the other fruits had stickers. She looked down at her special sticker and thought, "That must be the problem! She hated to give up her special sticker but if that was the reason the little boy wasn't choosing her, she felt that she must remove it.

When the little boy reached in and chose Hari, the pear, Pita burst into tears. Now her friend was gone and she felt more confused than ever. Hari was not round. What could possibly be so wrong with Pita?

That afternoon when it came time for a snack, the little boy's mother said, "Choose a snack from the fruit bowl."

The next morning, Hari was very concerned about Pita. "Pita, why are you bruised? Are you ok?"

Pita sighed, "I thought I could squish myself into a rounder shape and the little boy would finally choose me."

"Oh, Pita," said Hari, "you don't need to make yourself shinier or squish yourself into a rounder shape to be chosen for snack. Just be patient. You're still a bright banana and I know you'll be chosen soon."

After several minutes of trying, she hadn't been very successful and she had bruised herself in several places. She crawled back into the fruit bowl, feeling defeated.

She jumped out of the fruit bowl and began trying to wedge herself between the bowl and the wall. She was hoping she could squish herself into a rounder shape.

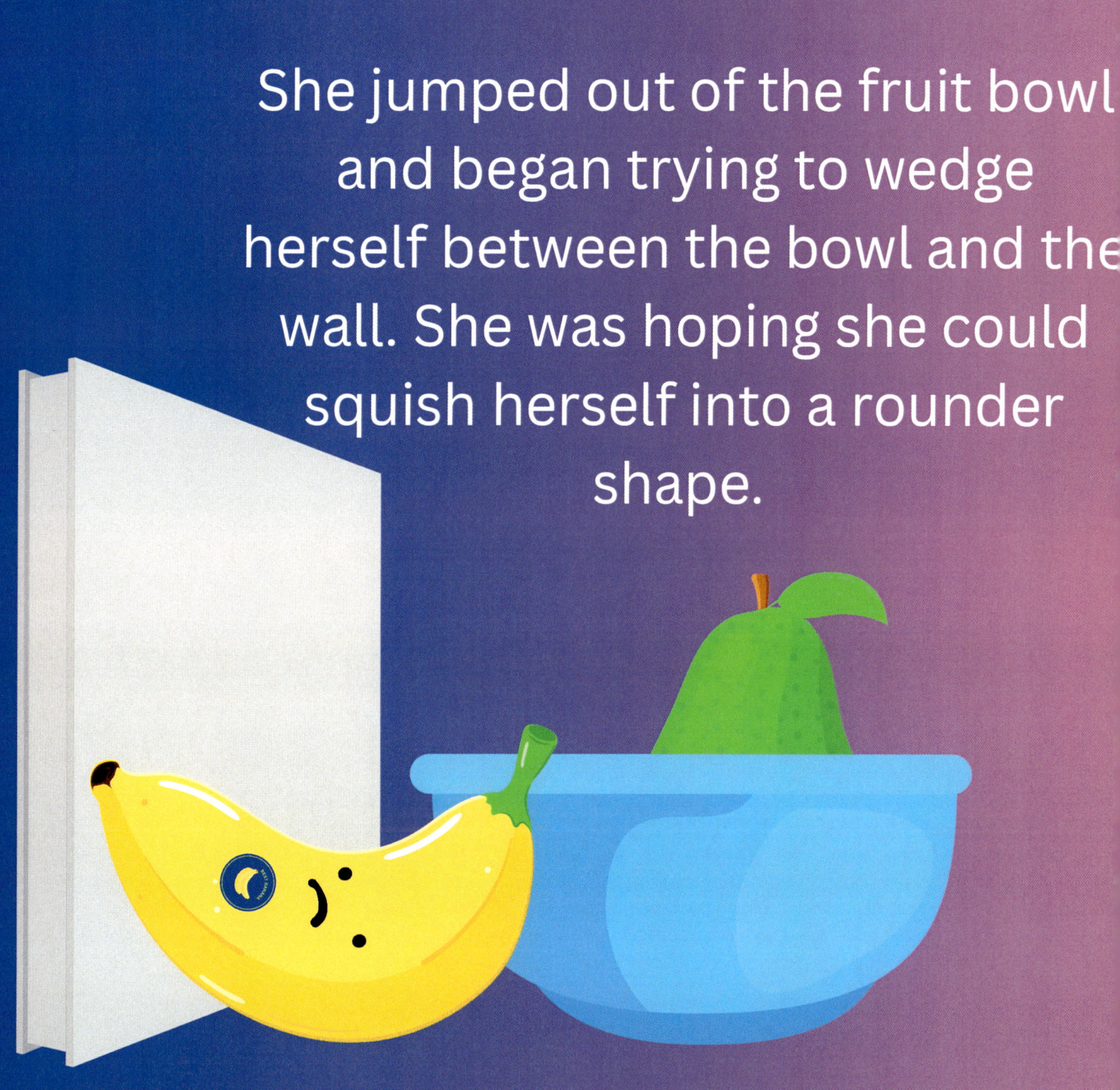

Pita thought it was very nice for Hari to say those things to her but she was still worried and couldn't fall asleep that night.

In the middle of the night, she had a sudden thought. The apple and orange were round! The only fruits left were her and Hari, the pear. They were different and more oblong shapes. That was surely what was wrong with Pita.

Hari saw that Pita was crying and asked, "Pita, why are you so sad?"

Pita said, "The little boy still hasn't chosen me. They said I was the brightest banana. I've tried to make myself shinier. I don't know why the little boy still won't choose me."

Hari smiled softly at Pita. "Pita, you ARE the brightest banana. You are big and ripe and you're a beautiful shade of yellow. I am sure that the little boy will choose you tomorrow."

"I don't understand what's wrong with me," Pita said with tears in her eyes to Hari, the kind faced pear.

Pita felt so sad and confused. She had been sure she would be chosen by the little boy today. She wondered what was wrong with her to make the little boy think she wasn't good enough to choose.

Then he reached in and chose the orange and was gone.

The little boy stood on his tip toes and peered into the blue bowl, letting his eyes rest on each of the pieces of fruit.

Finally, the little boy and his mother entered the cozy kitchen.

"Choose your snack for the day," his mother said.

The next day, Pita tried to keep a smile on her face while the fruit in the blue bowl waited for snack time. She kept checking her reflection in the bowl to see if she looked shinier and she took care to straighten her special sticker. She wanted to look her best.

Her sticker reminded her of when she was picked and they had called her the brightest banana. It helped her feel less sad. She didn't sleep much that night because she was worried about not being good enough for the little boy.

That night when the other fruits were sleeping, she jumped out of the fruit bowl and rolled back and forth on a nearby dish towel, trying to get her yellow peel to shine. She was careful not to rub off her special sticker.

Pita thought about what the orange said. This made her feel very sad. Maybe she wasn't the brightest banana. The apple was very shiny. Maybe she wasn't shiny enough for the little boy.

The sassy orange chuckled, "Maybe you were the brightest in your bunch. But there is more than one bunch of bananas. Maybe the little boy likes shiny fruit," the orange responded.

Pita slumped against the bowl, frowning. "I don't understand," she said, "I really thought he would choose me. They said I'm the brightest banana."

The apple gave a tiny squeal of excitement and smiled widely as he lifted him out. Then the boy was gone.

The little boy peered into the blue fruit bowl for a few seconds, looking intently at each fruit before finally reaching in and choosing the shiny, red apple.

When afternoon came, the little boy and his mother came to the cozy kitchen. "Choose a snack from the fruit bowl," his mother said.

Pita got excited too. She knew she'd be chosen. After all, she was the brightest banana.

The apple smiled and said excitedly, "We are waiting for the little boy to choose one of us. Every day, he takes a break from playing and comes to the kitchen for a snack."

She asked the other fruit, "What are we waiting for?"

Pita looked around at the other fruit in the blue bowl and everyone was different. There was a shiny red apple, a kind faced pear and a sassy orange in the bowl with her.

Pita wasn't just a bright banana. When she was picked from the tree, they called her the brightest and best banana and they put a sticker right on her peel. It made her feel special.

In a cozy kitchen, there was a large, blue bowl of fruit. One day, a bright banana named Pita found herself inside with many other kinds of fruit.